Mia Mayhem

#5

STOPS TIME!

BY **KARA WEST**   ILLUSTRATED BY **LEEZA HERNANDEZ**

LITTLE SIMON

New York   London   Toronto   Sydney   New Delhi

This book is a work of fiction. Any references to historical events, real people, or real places are used fictitiously. Other names, characters, places, and events are products of the author's imagination, and any resemblance to actual events or places or persons, living or dead, is entirely coincidental.

LITTLE SIMON

An imprint of Simon & Schuster Children's Publishing Division

1230 Avenue of the Americas, New York, New York 10020

First Little Simon paperback edition September 2019

Copyright © 2019 by Simon & Schuster, Inc.

Also available in a Little Simon hardcover edition

All rights reserved, including the right of reproduction in whole or in part in any form.

LITTLE SIMON is a registered trademark of Simon & Schuster, Inc., and associated colophon is a trademark of Simon & Schuster, Inc.

For information about special discounts for bulk purchases, please contact Simon & Schuster Special Sales at 1-866-506-1949 or business@simonandschuster.com.

The Simon & Schuster Speakers Bureau can bring authors to your live event.

For more information or to book an event contact the Simon & Schuster Speakers Bureau at 1-866-248-3049 or visit our website at www.simonspeakers.com.

Designed by Laura Roode

Manufactured in the United States of America 0819 MTN

2 4 6 8 10 9 7 5 3 1

Library of Congress Cataloging-in-Publication Data

Names: West, Kara, author. | Title: Mia Mayhem stops time! / Kara West ; illustrated by Leeza Hernandez. | Description: New York : Little Simon, 2019. | Series: Mia Mayhem ; 5 | Summary: "When Mia first learned she had superpowers, there was one ability that always came rather naturally: freezing time and people! So when she finally learns the secret to controlling it, she's excited to put her new skills to the test. But when she ends up accidentally freezing the entire town, will she find a way to make the clock start ticking again?"—Provided by publisher. | Identifiers: LCCN 2019022086 | ISBN 9781534449428 (paperback) | ISBN 9781534449435 (hc) | ISBN 9781534449442 (eBook)

Subjects: | CYAC: Superheroes—Fiction. | Time—Fiction. | African Americans—Fiction. | BISAC: JUVENILE FICTION / Action & Adventure / General. | JUVENILE FICTION / Readers / Chapter Books.

Classification: LCC PZ7.1.W43684 Mo 2019 | DDC [E]—dc23

LC record available at https://lccn.loc.gov/2019022086

CONTENTS

LATE AGAIN!

"Mia Macarooney, why are you late again?" asked Mrs. Cruz.

That was a very good question.

I was standing in her office as she wrote me another tardy slip. She was the principal of Normal Elementary School.

"Mia, this is the fourth time this week," she continued.

"I know. I'm sorry. I'll try to make sure it won't happen again," I replied.

Mrs. Cruz paused, waiting for me to say more.

But I couldn't make any hard promises.

Because every morning this week, weird things have happened to make me late. And I couldn't tell her why.

Why not, you ask?

Well, because . . . I've been using my superpowers!

Yeah, you heard me right.

My name is Mia, and *I. Am. A. Superhero!*

Right now, during regular school, I'm Mia Macarooney.

But when the school bell rings, I go by MIA MAYHEM.

I'm still really new at being super—that's why I go to the Program for In Training Superheroes, aka the PITS! The PITS is a top secret superhero-training academy. And thanks to the things I've learned, I've been able to save the day before school even starts!

On Monday, I flew up into a tree to help a squirrel who was afraid of heights.

On Tuesday, I helped an old lady cross a busy street.

Then on Wednesday, there was a bridge that got stuck in the up position.

And then this morning, my cat, Chaos, ran after the garbage truck!

So, yeah, in short, this week has been total mayhem.

I wish I could tell Mrs. Cruz the truth, but I need to protect my secret identity. There are only four people who know: my parents (who are also superheroes), Eddie (my best friend), and Dr. Sue Perb (the headmistress of the PITS).

That's why all I could do was apologize.

"Sorry again, Mrs. Cruz," I said, looking down at the floor.

"I know you are, Mia," Mrs. Cruz said. "But four tardies in one week means you'll have to make up your morning class after school today."

That was going to mess up my entire day!

Being a superhero and a regular kid took a lot of balance—I had a tight schedule to keep.

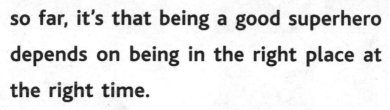

And if there is one thing I've learned so far, it's that being a good superhero depends on being in the right place at the right time.

But today, trying to do the right thing for others is bad news for me . . . because it looks like I'm going to be stuck in that makeup session, whether I like it or not.

CHAPTER 2

Saving Time

There are a lot of problems with getting to school late, and this one is the worst: When you walk into class, everyone turns and looks at you!

I tried to sneak in as quietly as I could, but all eyes were on me as I walked by. When I got to my desk, I swung my backpack off my shoulder. As soon as I did, I knew I was in trouble.

WHOOSH!

Being really strong is awesome. But controlling my strength is still tricky. I've broken my desk many times. And I was about to do it again.

But then something weird happened.

Somehow, without doing it on purpose, I went into *slow motion*.

Like for real!

I caught my backpack in time so that it wouldn't land so hard.

Then, before I knew it, time went back to normal speed!

I looked over at Eddie to see if he'd noticed. But he just waved as usual and didn't seem weirded out at all.

So I shrugged it off and hoped it was just a one-time glitch.

Luckily, the rest of the day went by smoothly. That is until we decided to play dodgeball at recess. It's my favorite game, and now that I have superspeed, I never get hit! That's not the only reason I like it, but it *is* a nice perk.

In the last five minutes of the game, Eddie and I were the only two people left on our team. I was on guard, ready to jump in either direction, when a kid threw a ball directly at Eddie!

I knew there was no way he was going to avoid it.

So I took a dive to my left to save him. And as I reached my arm out, the entire room froze.

Oh yeah. Before I go on, you should know that I have a habit of freezing my best friend. I've seen that shocked look on his face before. The thing is, this is the first time I've frozen a large group of people. So I'm not totally sure this trick will work.

I grabbed the ball, and time instantly started back up again.

Thank goodness.

In moments like these, I was really glad I was a superhero. So obviously, I *had* to do more time slowdowns after that. In the cafeteria, I saved a lunch lady from spilling a whole tray of food.

Then, back in class, I saved a kid from tripping over a chair. And I even made sure that our class gerbil, Lester, wouldn't eat his food too fast and get a stomachache!

Now, I have to admit that I wasn't exactly sure how I was doing it all. Controlling time wasn't a power I had learned at the PITS yet. It just came naturally.

All I knew was that secretly helping people was the best feeling ever!

By the end of the day, I was in such a good mood that nothing could bother me!

Done in a Flash!

Okay. Forget what I just said.

The after-school makeup session with Mrs. Cruz totally bothered me.

As soon as I walked into the classroom, I wished I could teleport to the PITS.

Why? Well, do you see that board? I have to do all those math problems! It's going to take *forever*!

I groaned as I pulled out a piece of paper and a pencil.

As I stared at the blank page, that's when I had the most incredible idea!

Now that I can control time, why not put it to good use?

If I paused this moment, then I could do all the work, hand it in, and still get to the PITS on time!

I reached out my hand, and like before, everything froze. Then I solved all the problems as quickly as I could.

When I was done, I walked up to the front and tapped my principal on the shoulder to start the clock again.

"Here's my work, Mrs. Cruz," I said.

"What? We just started the class a minute ago!" she cried. Then I saw her eyes get really big as she took my paper and scanned it.

"Well, I guess I work fast," I said with a shrug.

Mrs. Cruz looked at my paper and then back at me several times.

"Yes, I can't argue with that," she replied. "But I still have to review it before you can leave."

Harrumph.

This was an unexpected speed bump in my awesome time-saving plan.

And I didn't know a shortcut out of this one. So I sat there and waited while Mrs. Cruz checked my work.

It took forever.

Well, okay. It took only fifteen minutes. But still! That was fifteen minutes I could have spent in class at the PITS!

When the principal was finally done, she stamped "100%" at the top of the page.

"I still don't see how you did it," she said. "But great job!"

"Thanks, Mrs. Cruz!" I said, cramming the paper into my pocket as I headed for the door.

"Oh, Mia!" she called after me. "Remember, don't be late tomorrow!"

I nodded with a smile.

But the truth was that I had no idea what would happen in the morning.

For now, I was just worried about how I was going to sneak into my PITS class as quietly as possible.

CHAPTER
4

A NEW
DIRECTION

Thank goodness I know how to use
superspeed. It always helps when I'm
running late. I arrived at the front of the
PITS in record time.

First, I changed into my suit. Then I
turned the DO NOT ENTER sign and scanned
myself into the building.

The PITS looks like an empty
warehouse from the outside.

The dangling sign keeps regular people from trying to enter.

But on the inside, it's the coolest place ever! There are high-tech screens on every wall, and busy superheroes are running around all the time.

I sped through the main lobby, also known as the Compass, and I headed for the room where today's lesson was being held.

I put my ear against the door and listened.

Oh no! I totally picked the wrong day to be late.

Dr. Sue Perb, the headmistress of the school, was teaching a special Save the Day lesson.

I didn't want to walk into the room while she was talking.

So I reached my hand out in front of me. And just like that, all the movement

in the hallway and inside the classroom stopped.

Then I quickly snuck in and stood next to my two friends Penn Powers and Allie Oomph.

When I tapped Allie on the shoulder, she unfroze. Perfecto! It worked again! I smiled at her like I'd been there all along.

"And so," Dr. Perb continued, "that's today's exercise. Now let's all break into groups."

Oh no! That's when I realized there was a big problem.

I may have managed to sneak into class, but I didn't know what we were doing because I'd missed Dr. Perb's instructions.

Starting this lesson without knowing what do to was definitely a recipe for disaster.

Then again, I didn't want to ask Dr. Perb to repeat herself, and I couldn't ask Allie or Penn either. I wanted to keep this new secret to myself. At least for now.

I knew that freezing the clock wouldn't help this time.

Slowing down time wouldn't do anything either.

But maybe . . . what if I could *rewind* time? If I could go backward, maybe I could get to class before Dr. Perb started talking!

WHIRRRR!

First I froze everyone so they wouldn't see what I was doing. If I wanted try it, it was now or never.

But this time nothing happened.

So I did it again.

And again.

But still nothing.

Sweat started dripping down my face, so I took a deep breath. Then I closed my eyes, stretched my hand out, and thought of the exact moment I wanted to rewind to.

When I opened my eyes, I couldn't believe it.

I was back in my makeup session!

My Egg-cellent New Power

For real! I'm exactly back where I started.

Mrs. Cruz was sitting at the front desk, exactly like before! I wanted to jump up and cheer. But that would have been weird. After all, who gets excited about redoing a makeup class?

And in any case, I had to stay focused if I was going to get back to the PITS earlier than before.

I held out my hand, and as expected, everything froze.

Then I took out the crumpled piece of paper in my pocket and copied in all the answers.

A second later, I was back at Mrs. Cruz's desk.

"What? We just started the class a minute ago!" she cried. Then I saw her eyes get really big just like last time.

"Well, I guess I work fast," I repeated with a shrug.

"I can't argue with that," she said

with a smile. "But I still have to review it before you can leave."

Aha! I knew this was my chance! I couldn't wait *another* fifteen minutes. Especially since I knew the answers were correct.

So I put Mrs. Cruz on pause.

Then I grabbed the stamp from her desk, marked the page, and put it back in her hand before unfreezing her.

This time she looked even more confused. But in the end, my plan worked!

I dashed over to the PITS and was outside my classroom a whole fifteen minutes earlier than last time.

I took a deep breath and quietly snuck in.

"Today you will be doing your first Save the Day exercise," Dr. Perb began.

I grinned from ear to ear. I had come into class at the perfect time.

"You've all been learning how to use superpowers, but there's more to being a good superhero," Dr. Perb said. "It's important to be aware of what's going on around you. If you don't, you may miss your one chance to help someone."

Dr. Perb pointed to the tables set up in the center of the room.

"Today, your main mission is to complete these jigsaw puzzles!"

We looked at one another totally confused. That didn't seem very super at all.

But then Dr. Perb pushed a button on her watch, and a loud sound started blaring through the room.

"Of course, there's a catch. You will have to do the puzzle over this noise while also watching out for these eggs."

Eggs? Did she just say "eggs"?

She pushed her watch a second time.

This time, a hole in the wall opened
and a jumbo-size egg sailed across the
room.

Dr. Perb flew up and caught it gently,
right before it landed on a kid's head.

When she landed, we all cheered.

Our mission today was to keep the eggs from hitting us while finishing our puzzle in less than ten minutes. So we quickly split into groups, and we started fitting pieces together.

That's when out of nowhere, Penn flew into the air. Then he reached out to save me from getting hit with an egg!

I looked up and gave him a quick high five.

Phew! What a close call!

Right then, I saw something that Penn didn't: Another kid was about to barrel right into him!

So without thinking, I froze time, flew up, and nudged the kid so that she'd fly just past Penn.

It worked! Over and over again.

So for the rest of class, I secretly saved other kids from crashing into one another.

I knew it wasn't part of the lesson, but I couldn't help it! For the first time since I'd found out I was a superhero, I felt in total control.

And it felt egg-cellent.

CHAPTER 6

BOWLING TIME!

With this new awesome power, it was easy to stay on top of my packed schedule. This was really good news because today was day two of our Save the Day training with Dr. Perb.

"You'll be doing the same exercise as yesterday," she said, "except for one difference: Instead of eggs, we'll using bowling balls!"

She pushed a button on her watch.

A hole in the wall opened and a giant bowling ball came flying toward her! We watched in awe as she flew up and caught it.

"Keep your eyes open, everyone!" she warned. "You'll need to focus on your puzzle while using your strength, balance, and flying skills all at once."

As usual, Allie, Penn, and I were a team again today. Allie looked over at me with her game face on. She was wearing her awesome rocket blades. They were perfect for flying and getting from point A to point B in a flash.

I gave her a quick thumbs-up. Then
in a blink of an eye, things got crazy.

But luckily, after yesterday, I felt like a pro.

In fact, I froze time even when I didn't have to, just to practice my skills.

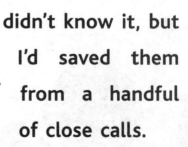

It was all going perfectly. Our puzzle was almost done, and we'd caught seven bowling balls among the three of us. My friends didn't know it, but I'd saved them from a handful of close calls.

Right then, Allie spotted a bowling ball and jetted up into the air. I froze time and flew up beside her, like I'd been doing all class.

But this time, something was wrong.

Allie was frozen, but the ball was still moving!

I quickly pushed her to the side. As soon as I touched her, the entire room unfroze.

And this time, I wasn't fast enough.

The bowling ball hit her, and one of her rocket blades totally came off!

"Hey! Are you girls okay?" Dr. Perb
called out as she flew up to us.

"Yeah, I'm okay. But Allie got hit!" I yelled out.

"Oh, it's easy to put back on," Allie said cheerfully. "See?"

Allie always had a good attitude. But I felt terrible. My friend almost got hurt because of me. And it was all my fault!

So for the rest of class, I stopped playing around.

Freezing time definitely had its perks, but it wasn't worth putting my friends in any danger.

CHAPTER 7

THE MISSION

After class, Allie, Penn, and I headed to our lockers.

"I'm sorry about earlier, Allie," I said.

"It's . . . no—thing. It's . . . no—thing," she replied.

I looked at her totally confused.

Allie kept moving back and forth, like she was on repeat. And so was Penn.

I had no idea what was going on.

"Hey, guys!" I yelled, waving. "Stop goofing around!"

But the next second, they were both completely frozen in place.

I thought I had stopped time again by mistake. So I touched Allie on the shoulder to restart things . . . but nothing happened.

I tried again.

And again.

Nothing.

Uh-oh. Did my powers stop working?

I looked around in a panic and realized it wasn't just my friends. Everyone else was on pause too!

I tried to calm down. There had to be a way to fix this.

And if there was anyone who could help, it was Dr. Perb. I checked Dr. Perb's office, the gym, and everywhere in between. But she was nowhere to be found!

Was I really the only unstuck superhero in this entire school?

What was I going to do?

Tired, sweaty, and out of ideas, I headed back to where my friends were.

When I opened my locker, that's when I saw it. There was a box with a label that read: ONLY OPEN IN AN EMERGENCY.

Emergency? Yeah, I was definitely in the middle of one.

I opened the box. Inside, there was a top secret device with a video message—from Dr. Perb!

"Hello, Mia," she began. "If you're watching this, then my suspicions are correct—you are a Time Controller and your powers have gotten you into trouble. Not only have you frozen everyone inside the PITS, but I'm afraid the whole town needs your help."

Did she just say the whole town?

"Yes, that is correct. The entire town is now on pause," she went on as if she had heard me. "But don't panic. The good news is that when the gears of time get stuck, they can be undone by a Time Controller, like you!"

"But how?" I asked.

"That's a good question!" Dr. Perb cried, without missing a beat. "There is a special clock grease that time itself protects. You will need to coat the gears of time, located at the center of everything, to bring things back to normal again."

Oh boy. That was a lot of responsibility. And it didn't help that I had no idea what she was talking about.

But Dr. Perb wasn't done, so I listened as carefully as I could.

"One last thing before I go: Enclosed are two watches. When worn, they will unfreeze two people. Choose wisely because the fate of the PITS—and our town—rests with you."

I shook the box. Two high-tech watches that looked like the one that Dr. Perb always wore fell out.

Thankfully, I knew exactly who I was going to give them to.

CHAPTER
8

THE SEARCH

I turned and strapped the watches onto Allie and Penn. And just like that, they immediately became unstuck.

"Whoa!" said Penn, shaking his head.

"What just happened?" asked Allie.

"Are we in danger?" asked Penn.

"Is the PITS under attack?" asked Allie.

"No, everything is okay," I said.

"Well, it's not okay *yet*, but it will be. We're going to fix it."

"Fix what?" asked Allie.

"It's my fault," I said. Then I took a deep breath and told them everything,

I waited quietly. I knew they would be mad.

But Allie broke into a huge smile.

"Mia, that's so cool!" she cried. "I mean, except for freezing everybody, obviously. But we can fix that! What do we do first?"

"We need to find a special clock grease," I said. "The problem is that I don't know where it is. All Dr. Perb said was that time protected it."

None of us knew what that meant. But if there was anything super-important hidden anywhere, it had to be somewhere inside this building, right? After all, we were in the most high-tech, top secret building in town.

So we looked everywhere. And I mean EVERYWHERE.

But as we ran around, I started to get worried. I realized we didn't even know what we were looking for!

"What if we can't get time unstuck?" I asked, turning to Allie.

"We'll figure it out," Allie reassured me.

"Yeah," said Penn. "We'll solve it.

Remember what Dr. Perb said. We just need to be in the right place at the right time."

I supposed they were right. The only problem was that we had no idea where that place was. We were standing in the Compass, in the middle of a bunch of frozen superheroes.

I looked down at the floor as I let out a sigh.

And that's when it happened.

The big compass on the floor suddenly lit up! And it was pointing to the exit.

In that exact moment, I just remembered something Dr. Perb had told me on my very first day at the PITS. She had said that if I ever got lost, all I would need to do was go to the heart of the PITS.

And this was it! The compass was telling us where to go.

"Guys!" I yelled. "Look!"

I pointed at the compass, and Allie and Penn gasped.

Then I thought hard.

What had Dr. Perb meant by the center of everything? Was it the town hall? The park? The post office?

None of them felt right.

All these were common places to go, but there was only one thing at the center of town.

And just like that, everything clicked into place.

CHAPTER 9

The Hands
of Time

I knew exactly where we needed to go, so Penn and Allie followed my lead. As we flew through the air, I finally had a moment to look down.

Dr. Perb was right. The whole town really was frozen. Cars were stuck on the road, and people on the sidewalk were on pause too. There was even a dog that was frozen on his hind legs!

Oh boy. I have definitely gotten myself in some mayhem before. But pausing the entire town? This one definitely tops it all.

Moments later, we were finally in front of a tall stone clock tower in the center of town.

The hands of the clock had stopped moving.

So I did the most obvious thing first.
I flew over and tried to push them.

But it didn't work. Even though I
was using all my strength!

"How about if all three of us push?"
suggested Penn.

"Good idea! Three superheroes are stronger than one!" agreed Allie.

The three of us pushed together. And Allie even turned on her rocket blades! But it was no use. The hands didn't move one bit.

Right then, Penn flew up and called over.

"Hey, guys! There's a window up here!" he said, swooping through it.

When Allie and I got inside, my jaw dropped to the floor.

There were metal gears on every wall. Some gears were teeny tiny and some were enormous. Yet, somehow, they all fit together perfectly. I had never seen anything like it.

Right in the middle of the room, there was a set of steps that went up to a small platform.

I walked up to the top. At the center of the stage, there was a small round glass case.

I knew immediately that this was what I was looking for. The clock grease has been inside and guarded by the clock this whole time.

I blew the dust off and carefully lifted it up.

Inside, there was a big blue glass bottle with a set of oil containers.

"Hmm, what are we supposed to do with that?" Allie asked.

"We need to put oil on the clock hands and the gears, too," I said confidently.

In that moment, I realized that as a Time Controller there were things I knew without being told. I poured a little of the grease into Allie and Penn's containers. There was just enough for the three of us.

"Okay, guys. I'm going to pour this

directly onto the clock hands," I said.
"You both stay inside and grease the
gears from here."

Again, my friends took my lead, and
then I flew out the window.

After every inch of the clock was
covered, I counted to three.

And then we all pushed the gear
lever as hard as we could.

But still, nothing changed.

So I pushed even more as beads of
sweat trickled down my face.

Just when I wanted
to give up, a loud
screeching noise
began. Then soon
the cold metal
hands of the clock
lifted up and
started ticking.

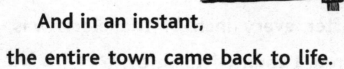

And in an instant,
the entire town came back to life.

IN DUE TIME

Wow!

Do you hear that?

Until now, I hadn't realized how quiet everything had been. When time was on hold, the entire outside world had been quiet.

But now that things were back to normal, the noise of car horns, laughter, and people talking filled the air.

Mission accomplished!

Well, almost accomplished. Before we celebrated, there was one more place we needed to check. We flew back to the PITS building and scanned ourselves in.

We walked inside the Compass, and that's when I finally let out a sigh of relief. The place was bustling with busy superheroes, just like always!

Penn, Allie, and I gave one another a high five. We really did it!

I carefully unlocked the watches from their wrists. It was time to return these devices back to their rightful owner, so we said good-bye, and I made my way to Dr. Perb's office.

I was so relieved that everything seemed to be back to normal. But I was nervous to see Dr. Perb face-to-face. At the door, I took a deep breath and knocked three times.

"Yes, come in, Mia," she called.

Then I walked in and put the two watches on her desk. "Thank you for these," I said quietly.

She had a serious, concerned look on her face.

So for a moment, I braced myself for the worst.

But instead, her eyes softened as she broke into a huge smile.

"Well done, Mia!" she cried. "I knew you would figure out where to go. Fixing time-control glitches is all about being at the right place at the right time. Take it from one Time Controller to another."

I looked at her with wide eyes.

"You mean, you're a—"

"Yes, I'm a Time Controller too. That's how I recognized what was going on with you during class. It's a very special power, and one I'm quite fond of using."

I smiled, finally relaxing a bit.

"Now, of course, we'll just have to set up some makeup sessions starting on Monday," she continued.

"Makeup sessions?" I asked.

"You were late to class yesterday," she replied matter-of-factly. "You didn't think I missed that, did you?"

What? No way!

Well, lesson learned! Never try to fool Dr. Perb, that's for sure!

I have no idea what a PITS makeup session will be like. But there's no use worrying about that. For now, I'm going to slow down and think about one of the coolest takeaways from this whole adventure: I, Mia Mayhem, am a Time Controller! While there are definitely some kinks I need to work out, can you believe it?

Now, I don't know what the future holds . . . but once I get a handle of things, I have a good feeling I'll find out . . . in due time.

Saturdays are my favorite. Whether it's watching cartoons or playing games, the weekends usually begin at my best friend Eddie's house.

I said hello to his parents, and then I walked into Eddie's room like I have done a hundred times before. This

Excerpt from *Mia Mayhem vs. the Mighty Robot*

time, though, I was in for the biggest surprise.

There was a robot as tall as me, standing in the middle of the room!

"Oh, hi, Mia!" Eddie cried. "You're right on time. I'm almost done with my latest invention!"

I circled the robot to get a better look. It was exactly our height, and on its front panel, there were big metal letters that spelled JR.

"Wow! You made a life-size robot!" I said, and my jaw dropped to the floor.

My best friend was really smart, and he loved robots.

"Yup! I named him Junior, and he's going to be my new helper. When I'm done, he should be able to help me with, well, everything!"

I leaned in to touch the robot's metal hand. And as soon as my grip tightened, his entire arm snapped off!

"Oh, sorry, Eddie! Sometimes I still can't control my strength," I said with a shrug.

"Don't worry about it. The arm was already loose," he replied.

I gave Eddie a little smile. I knew he was used to my mayhem by now.

Excerpt from *Mia Mayhem vs. the Mighty Robot*